UGLY DOLLS

THE MOVIE NOVEL

centum

UGLYDOLLS: THE MOVIE NOVEL

A CENTUM BOOK 978-1-913072-99-5

Published in Great Britain by Centum Books Ltd

This edition published 2019

1 3 5 7 9 10 8 6 4 2

Centum Books Ltd, 20 Devon Square, Newton Abbot,
Devon, TQ12 2HR, UK

books@centumbooksltd.co.uk

CENTUM BOOKS Limited Reg. No. 07641486

A CIP catalogue record for this book is available
from the British Library.

Printed in United Kingdom.

UGLY DOLLS

THE MOVIE NOVEL

Adapted by Arden Hayes
Screenplay by ALISON PECK
Story by ROBERT RODRIGUEZ

CHAPTER 1

The sun rose over Uglyville, and birdsong filled the air. In a tiny Ugly house on a tiny Ugly street, an UglyDoll named Moxy was still fast asleep. Her friend Peggy the Pegacorn flew by her window and let out her signature crowing sound.

"Wake up, Moxy!" Peggy cried.

Moxy's cute, buggy eyes blinked open. She threw back her blankets and ran over to the calendar on her wall. *Today's the day!* was scribbled on each of the previous days, but then was subsequently crossed out. She picked up her marker and wrote, *Today's the day!* one more time on the tenth of the month. This day was going to be different from all the others – she had a good feeling about it.

She twirled around her bedroom, glancing at

her reflection in the mirror on the wall. "*Hello, gorgeous*," she sang to herself.

> "Let's check out how you look today.
> Short and stubby,
> Nubby teeth out on full display!
> You're pinkish red,
> Got this thing on your head,
> And, whoa—
> Girl, you couldn't look better!"

Just then Ugly Dog, her sweet puppy pal, appeared at her window. "You're in a good mood!" he smiled.

"That's because today I'm going to get chosen to…"

"…Get chosen to go to the Big World and be with your child." Ugly Dog finished her sentence. "You say that every day."

"I know, but today I might be right," Moxy said. If you haven't noticed, Moxy was by far the most optimistic UglyDoll in Uglyville. When the sun wasn't shining, she was glad to have the shade. When her rickshaw broke down, she thought of it as the perfect opportunity to enjoy a walk through the village. When each day passed and she wasn't chosen to be with her child, Moxy knew the time she spent alone would make meeting her child that much sweeter. Nothing could spoil Moxy's good mood.

Moxy ran to her computer and typed up the latest edition of *The Daily Ugly*. The headline read, *Today's the Day!* She grabbed a stack and slid down her banister, ready to spread the good news. Ugly Dog was right behind her as she bounded out the door.

"*Call it hope or faith or whatever,*" she sang, twirling around. She handed out the newsletter to every Uglyville citizen she passed. "*I just know in my heart it's the day I've waited for forever!*"

Moxy skipped and danced through the streets, her heart light. She loved her colourful town and all the colourful, eccentric dolls in it. She loved the bizarre bright blue-and-yellow house that looked as if it were built upside down and the bakery with the lopsided awning. She loved the scooters and the carts and…well, everything.

"*Call it crazy,*" she sang, jumping on her bicycle. Ugly Dog sped up beside her on his skateboard. "*And yet – is there anything better than this? Life just couldn't be better than this!*"

They turned the corner and spotted Ox, the town's mayor, in one of Uglyville's biggest parks. He was hard to miss because he was bright green with two giant ears, and he was missing one eye. His good friend Lucky Bat was beside him, holding a shovel. Lucky Bat was the town's healer. He had pointy ears and a yellow superhero cape and was the most laid-back UglyDoll of all.

"Here ya go, Mayor Ox!" Moxy said, handing him a newsletter. "Hot off the press!"

"Thanks, Moxy," Ox replied. "Today's the day."

"You really think so?" Moxy smiled. "When

someone gets chosen, do they get picked up by, like, a big, long stretch dune buggy or something fancy?"

"I'm talking about the tree-planting ceremony," Ox said flatly.

Moxy tried to hide her disappointment as Lucky Bat helped plant Mr. Tree. The UglyDoll climbed into a hole, and Lucky Bat patted down the dirt around him. Then Lucky Bat snapped a few pictures to mark the occasion.

"Now, I've told you before," Ox went on. "All this business about the so-called Big World and children…it's just a fairy tale. Like the Easter Button or Santa Cloth."

"Everyone says that," Moxy tried. "But what's the harm in believing?"

"*Never mind that*," Ox sang. Whenever Moxy brought up the outside world, he tried to change the subject. He was always so upbeat, but he refused to think about children and love and what life would be like in the Big World.

"I'll tell you what the day will bring…
First a shindig, then a bash,
Then more partying.
Top it all with a rave, then a ball—
You know it couldn't be better!"

Ox found any reason to celebrate. Moxy sometimes thought of him more as an Uglyville party planner than a mayor, because he was always dreaming up some new event. Annual Cupcake Day, the Midnight Magic Show, or Ballet in the Park – he'd planned every crazy event you could think of.

Moxy and Ugly Dog went on their way, accepting ice-cream pies from Wage, the town's best baker, as they left. Moxy knew Ox was right. Even if she never got to the Big World, Uglyville was a beautiful place to be – and spectacularly fun, too.

She sang:

"Yes, it's a square-peg life in a round-hole town,
But the folks couldn't be any sweeter.

It may be upside-backward
And wrong-side down,
But it just couldn't be more completer!"

"*And there's so much to do,*" her friend Babo joined in.

"*And it's all such bliss,*" Wage sang.

Then they belted out the last line together: "*No, it couldn't get better than…*"

Before they could finish their song, an alarm blared. "Incoming! Incoming!"

"Come on, UglyDolls," Peggy the Pegacorn shouted as she flew into the air. "New arrival!"

All the dolls in Uglyville stopped what they were doing and ran to the high cliff at the edge of town. A giant sunflower grew there. Its face was tilted up towards the sky. Everyone cleared a path so Ox could get through to the front of the crowd.

"New UglyDoll coming in hot!" Ox yelled. "Willard, shake a leg!"

A large, slow UglyDoll shuffled forward. He had

a mattress tied to his back as he walked towards the target sign painted on the ground. But before he could get there, the UglyDolls heard a loud *POP!* and a jagged-headed UglyDoll came flying out from the centre of the sunflower. She just barely missed Willard as she landed head first on the patchwork ground.

"Willard, you are a real disappointment," Ugly Dog said.

"And that's just one of your amazing qualities!" Babo cried, a genuine smile on his face.

The rest of the crowd was too busy staring at the new UglyDoll to notice Babo and Ugly Dog. The plush doll was lying face down. Ox went to her and offered one of his long ears. The little doll reached out and took it, pulling herself up. She was still a bit dazed, but when she stood, they saw the real problem.

Moxy gasped. The doll's head had been smashed flat. It looked as if she had a thick, triangular, wedge-shaped head, with one single eyeball in the centre of it. She lifted that eyeball and stared out at the crowd.

"Is this where I get chosen for the Big World?" the doll asked. Then she smiled, revealing two sharp fangs.

CHAPTER 2

Ugly Dog spent the afternoon giving Wedgehead a tour of every wild and weird spot in Uglyville. They went to the milkshake fountain and the skateboard park and then the Swirly Twirly Playground, where every ride made you dizzy. When they were finished with the tour, the entire town came together for a feast to celebrate the new arrival.

Babo pulled a lever and Main Street transformed into a dining table. It was so long that every UglyDoll could sit together for dinner. Legs the octopus passed heaping plates of plush food down the row, letting each doll help themselves. There was every kind of delicacy you could imagine – dumplings, coconut buns, blueberry cakes and more.

Because it was Uglyville, it wasn't long before the group was singing and laughing and hurling their food in a fun, impromptu food fight. Moxy ducked away from the crowd so she wouldn't get hit.

Her friends were right – it couldn't get better than this. But then why couldn't she stop thinking about what happened at the sunflower today? Why were Wedgehead's first words about the Big World?

"You see, Moxy?" Ox strolled up beside her with Lucky Bat. "It doesn't get better than this."

The food fight had become even wilder since they stepped away. Every doll was laughing and throwing strawberries and sticky buns at one another. Even Wedgehead had joined in the fun. A spring onion pancake was covering her one eye.

"I love it here." Moxy smiled. "But don't you think it's weird that every new doll comes here knowing about the Big World? That must mean something, right?"

Ox shook his head. He sometimes got frustrated

that Moxy always wanted to talk about the Big World, and children, and what was beyond Uglyville.

"Don't miss out on everything in front of you for a pipe dream," he finally said. "Promise me you'll give up this Big World thing."

Give up this Big World thing? Was Ox really serious? If there *was* a child out there for her, Moxy would never be able to give up searching for her. She'd never stop wondering how she could get to the Big World and her new life.

"Sure, I promise," Moxy finally said. But she was crossing her stubby pink fingers behind her back. As she walked away, Ox called out after her.

"You're not going to give it up, are you?" he asked.

"Not a chance," she called back.

Ox and Lucky Bat stood there, watching as Moxy joined the rest of her friends. Within minutes, she was chucking coconut buns and milkshakes and laughing in the midst of the food fight.

"We all have our dreams," Lucky Bat offered. "Remember how long you tried to pull off that fedora?"

Ox had worn it for an entire year. It looked so silly, jammed between his ears. Lucky Bat had gently suggested he retire it for something a little more "him," but Ox refused. He just kept pretending he didn't understand what Lucky Bat meant.

Besides, Ox thought it made him look debonair.

"But *her* dream is a fantasy!" Ox said. "The longer she takes to accept that, the greater the heartbreak will be." Then he stared off into the distance. "And I *did* pull off that fedora."

"Situations like this usually need to be handled delicately," Lucky Bat continued. He was always offering advice, even if he didn't mean to.

"Well, I don't know anyone around here who

handles things more delicately than you," Ox said. "I'll send Moxy over to your place tomorrow."

"What could *I* say if an entire song can't convince her?" Lucky Bat asked. Hadn't they sung that it couldn't get better than this? They must've done about a hundred refrains of that very verse.

"Just gently nudge her in the right direction," Ox went on. "But forcefully. Because remember: Moxy's entire future and emotional well-being is riding on exactly what you say."

"Ah…" Lucky Bat suddenly felt an intense amount of pressure. Moxy had believed in the Big World for her whole entire life. It wasn't exactly going to be easy to convince her it didn't exist.

"Good luck!" Ox chirped. Then he smiled and rejoined the party.

The sun set over Uglyville and all the dolls had left the feast. Some had gone to launch fireworks by the lake, while others were preparing for another colourful day tomorrow. Babo and Wedgehead talked about making paper airplanes and flying them off Babo's roof.

Moxy walked back to her Ugly house, singing to herself as she went. "*Guess another sun has set and another moon has smiled. I'm still just one more doll still waiting for her child,*" she sang sadly as she climbed the stairs to her room.

She turned to the calendar on her wall, studying all the days she'd X-ed off. Every single one said *Today's the day!* in marker, but every single one of those days had come and gone, and Moxy still hadn't gone to the Big World.

"*I'm sure it's going to happen, just like the stories say…*" she sang. "*There's a new day 'round the corner. And it just might be the day.*"

Moxy drew a big X on her calendar, marking the end of the day. Then she climbed into bed and looked out at the fireworks exploding in the sky. Mayor Ox could say whatever he wanted, but Moxy would never give up hope.

Her child was out there somewhere. One day, they'd meet, even if it wasn't today, tomorrow, or the next day. She was sure of it.

CHAPTER 3

"Take that! And that!" Lucky Bat yelled as he soared through the air. The wind unfurled his long cape. Clouds rushed by, and he manoeuvred over and under them, trying to get a better view of the world below. "*Pow! Whoosh! Kapow!* I'm flying at speeds you can't even detect!"

He kept going, twisting this way and that, but the clothes hanger he was balanced on was digging into his round belly. On the stove, a teakettle let off some more steam. It filled the tiny wood house, becoming the clouds in his imaginary sky. A paper fan contraption created the wind that billowed his cape. Sometimes, if he squinted a little bit, he really did feel as if he were flying.

"Lucky Bat? Hello?" a familiar voice called.

He jumped off the hanger and ran out to the balcony railing. Moxy was at the front door. Had she heard him pretending to be a superhero? Had she seen his clothes-hanger contraption?

"Were you meditating?" she asked.

He let out a deep breath, relieved. "Yes, ha-ha," he laughed. "Yes, meditating. That is exactly what I was doing!"

"I bet you can tell something's on my mind," Moxy said as she ducked inside the house.

Lucky Bat shrugged, as if he were used to knowing all the secrets of the universe. As if he hadn't just been inside, teetering on a clothes hanger, pretending he could fly.

"I was concentrating on the sound of the wind," he said serenely.

"You're so wise," Moxy went on as Lucky Bat arranged a tray with two teacups. "You must know exactly what I'm here to talk to you about…"

Lucky Bat just nodded and poured the tea. He found that being the wise healer of the town really meant being quiet and pretending he was always pondering life's big questions.

"Every day I think, *Today's the day*," Moxy said sadly. "And then it isn't. And that's fine, it is, but... look, I've always believed the Big World is real. I know I'll find the perfect kid for me. But lately I'm starting to wonder... with no evidence, no proof..." She bit her lip with her three front teeth, unsure of herself. "What if it's... not true?"

Lucky Bat wasn't quite sure what to say. If Ox was so determined to dissuade Moxy from dreaming about the Big World, Lucky Bat wasn't going to be the doll to do it for him. Moxy deserved to have hope, didn't she? Who was he to crush it?

Lucky Bat reached into his cape and pulled out a fortune cookie from dinner three nights before. He'd been saving it for a midnight snack, but he thought that maybe – just maybe – this would be a good time to use it. He found that fortune cookies sometimes offered the most profound guidance. That, and they were delicious.

He cracked it open and tugged the tiny piece of paper out.

"Hmmm..." he said, reading it. *"Find your own truth! 6, 9, 25, 18, 36, 41..."*

Moxy stared straight ahead, trying to figure out what it all meant.

"Wow," she finally said. "This is why you're the wisest doll in town. You're so right. I have to believe in myself."

"Uhhh..." Lucky Bat put on his best *Zen Master* face. "Sure."

"So how do I do that? Specifically?" Moxy asked.

Lucky Bat didn't know. Everyone thought he was so wise, but it wasn't as if he could see the future or anything. You'd be surprised how far he'd got by smiling and saying nothing at all. He poured Moxy some more tea, hoping to stall for time.

"Oh! You want to read my tea leaves!" Moxy said, peering into her cup. "Of course."

She chugged the tea in less than two seconds and then tried to hand the cup to Lucky Bat.

"Reading tea leaves is not really my thing," Lucky Bat said. He fumbled with his words, trying to figure out what he could offer her. "But I can tell you your forehead looks nice and bright, just like always!"

Nothing would stop Moxy, though. She slid the empty cup in front of him and leaned in close. "What do you see?" she whispered.

"U-uh…" Lucky Bat stuttered. "You…"

"*You*," Moxy repeated. She paused, pondering his word choice. Everything seemed like a clue. "Oh, you mean *me*. It's not what *you* see but what *I* see?"

Lucky Bat was silent.

She stared down at the cup. "I see leaves… *leaves*! I need to *leave*! I need to find *proof*. All this time I've been waiting for my child to find me. But I should go and find my child!"

Lucky Bat just stared at his nubby little hands. If that was what Moxy saw, who was he to correct her?

She pushed her chair out and stood, dizzy with her new revelation. She could barely look at

Lucky Bat, she was so excited. After all these days of waiting and wondering and hoping, she finally had a plan.

"Thank you so much, Lucky!" she called as she headed for the door. "You always know just what to say!"

CHAPTER 4

Lucky Bat followed Moxy out of the teahouse, trying to explain that maybe Moxy *shouldn't* run away from Uglyville on a quest to find her child. Couldn't she see something else in the tea leaves, like an arrow pointing back towards her house or an octagonal stop sign?

"Uh, Moxy," he said. "I think you may have misinterpreted the spirit of what I was trying to..."

"Ugly Dog, wake up!" Moxy called out. Her furry friend was napping on his porch. His one eye blinked open, and he followed her and Lucky Bat across the street.

Moxy was practically skipping. She peered into every house and shop she passed, looking for more dolls to share the good news with. Babo climbed down a ladder outside of Wage's bakery. He was a giant grey doll with short, stubby legs.

"Babo!" she yelled. "Lucky Bat has a great new idea!"

"No, no, no, no…" Lucky Bat whispered to himself, but everyone was already too excited to hear him.

"We're gonna make all our dreams come true!" Moxy said cheerfully. She knocked on the door of the bakery. Wage was usually inside, baking something delicious. "Wage!" Moxy called. "Today's the day!"

Lucky Bat hovered behind her, trying to get her attention. "We should really consult Ox…" he tried. Ox had told him to talk some sense into Moxy, to lead her away from her Big World dreams – this was definitely not what he'd had in mind.

Wage grabbed some doughnuts and ice-cream cakes and followed the rest of the group outside. Lucky Bat jumped in front of them and waved his cape and stomped his feet, but no one seemed to notice. The enthusiasm train had left the station, and there was no way to stop it now. More dolls were climbing on board.

The group bounded down the street together, chomping on some of the desserts along the way. Ox was coming out of the sweet shop when he spotted them. He licked a giant red lollipop.

"Oh, hello, Moxy!" he said cheerfully. "You look like you all are having a good time."

Lucky Bat cringed. *Just keep walking; just keep walking*, he thought, trying to will everyone away from Ox.

"Yep!" Moxy said. "I spoke to Lucky Bat, and he made everything clear!"

"Hey, atta-bat," Ox said, giving Lucky Bat two thumbs up.

Lucky Bat followed the crowd down the street, trying to get away from Ox as fast as he could. He couldn't tell Ox he'd failed. He couldn't tell him he'd actually *inspired* Moxy to look for this imaginary future child, rather than dissuade her.

Moxy stopped at the base of the giant cliff and stared up at the giant sunflower on top of it. "Everything that comes to Uglyville arrives here.

Sooo…if we're going to find the Big World, it's only logical we start here."

"Okay…" said Wage, a cute orange doll who wore her blue bakery apron wherever she went and was the most practical of the group. If Ox told Moxy to forget about this silly dream, then Wage thought Moxy should forget about this silly dream. "The Big World and children. Do. Not. Exist. But I have a feeling you're going to ignore me and–"

"I just want to have a look inside that flower!" Moxy cried. "Who's with me?"

"Yep, she just ignored me," Wage muttered.

Moxy turned around, looking at the small crowd that had followed her. She raised her arms, waiting for someone to join her, but Wage and Lucky Bat just stared straight ahead.

"I'm in," Ugly Dog said. He smiled and stepped forward.

"Me too," Babo said.

Two down, two to go. Moxy would not give up hope. She stood there, holding her pose, waiting for the others to join her. How could they not want to see what was inside that sunflower? How did they not want to know, once and for all, about the Big World and children?

"Come on, come on," Moxy urged. She refused to put down her arms.

Finally, Lucky Bat and Wage gave in and stepped forward to join the others.

"We're in," they said together.

"Yes!" Moxy cheered. "You guys are the Ugly-est!"

(That was the highest praise coming from Moxy.)

Babo glanced at the sunflower. "And we know just how to get up there…"

"We do?" Ugly Dog asked.

He stood there, trying to figure out what Babo was talking about. How were they going to get all the way up to the sunflower? It was, like, a million miles away from them.

"You'd have to get something up there that could grip onto the edge and support all our weight. That would be crazy," Ugly Dog said, keeping his eyes locked on the flower. A minute passed and no one responded. When he turned around, everyone was staring right at him. "Oh no, no, no, no, no, no. Let me tell you this: I don't know what you're thinking, but I'm not doing it."

But Babo and Wage and Moxy and Lucky Bat just kept smiling.

It was too late. They'd already decided on a plan.

CHAPTER 5

Ahhhhhhhh!" Ugly Dog was hurtling through the air, his mouth wide as he headed straight towards the giant sunflower. Its petals opened as he neared it, and he bit down hard on one of them. A long rope was tied to his leg.

"Anytime now, guys," he said through clenched teeth. "Let's go."

Babo climbed up the rope first, then the rest of the dolls followed. Ugly Dog felt as if his whole body were being stretched to its breaking point. One by one, they squirmed over his head and into the flower's centre. Now that they could see the fake flower up close, it was obvious it was just an entrance to a hollow metal pipe. Ahead of them was a long tunnel that faded into darkness.

"So this is what the inside of a flower looks like?" Ugly Dog asked.

"This is where my nightmares are made," Wage

said, and she was only half kidding. It was terrifying
– there was no way she was going inside. "All right,
that's it. Let's go."

Wage turned around, leading the others away
from the tunnel. They would just climb down
the rope and go back to Uglyville and their safe
little lives and forget all about this Big World
nonsense. That was reasonable. That made
perfect sense.

But Moxy stepped into the pitch-black tunnel.
Then she took another step.

"Let's just call it a day, huh?" Babo laughed
nervously. He was frozen, watching as Moxy moved
further inside.

"You guys," Moxy insisted. "This pipe goes
somewhere."

"Say something to her," Wage whispered to
Lucky Bat.

"Umm…" Lucky Bat tried to think. "Sometimes,
the insides of our dreams are hollow. Like this pipe,
for example."

Moxy nodded. She stood there for a moment, taking in Lucky Bat's advice. Then she charged ahead, screaming. "*Ahh!* I just gotta see what it's like! Here I go!"

Wage ran in after her. "Moxy! Moxy, slow down; it's dangerous!"

The pipe slowly slanted upwards and Moxy sprinted ahead, but the sides of it were slippery. She ran forward and slid back down, then tried it once more. She'd need help if she wanted to go any further.

"Guys, what if this is the way to the Big World?" she asked, turning around to face her friends.

Babo looked doubtful. "But Ox says there's no Big World and he…"

"He didn't know there was something else out there!" Moxy tried. "But we do. This pipe, it's real. And it has to lead somewhere. Maybe it's the Big World. If anyone can figure it out, it's us. Lucky Bat, you're so curious about the mysteries of life. Hello! Mystery ahead!"

"Hmm," Lucky Bat murmured. "I suppose a little journey *could* be enlightening."

The rest of the dolls agreed. Ugly Dog would never let Moxy go alone; he had always been Moxy's best friend. And Babo could never say no to someone who needed help, especially someone he loved as much as Moxy.

"This is ridiculous!" Wage tried. "Going into a creepy pipe when it spells certain doom? Err...no. No, thank you!".

"Wage..." Moxy started.

"Go ahead! Give me your big sell, Moxy!" Wage was getting really worked up. "Tell me that I have to go. Tell me that it's my duty as a doll to be a friend; tell me that deep down I want to know what's over there, too. Come on, give me the pitch!"

Moxy took a deep breath and looked right at her dear friend. "If you don't come, you're going to have to climb down that cliff all by yourself."

Wage turned and saw how high up they were. They must've been hundreds of feet above the ground. Uglyville was just a tiny speck beneath them.

"Good pitch," Wage finally said. Then she started ahead into the tunnel. "Let the record show that I'm against this."

Moxy, Babo and Ugly Dog followed along behind her. Moxy glanced sideways at Ugly Dog, and the two shared a smile.

"Now, that's what I'm talking about, Wage!" Ugly Dog called out. Then he ran forward into the darkness.

CHAPTER 6

They'd been walking in the dark for more than an hour. Moxy had hoped Lucky Bat had some sort of bat sonar or something to help them find the way, but apparently he wasn't that kind of bat. They just kept trudging forward, completely lost.

"I have a flashlight," Babo's voice called out from behind Moxy.

"A flashlight?" Wage asked. "So why have we been walking in the dark for the last hour, then?"

"Well, Lucky Bat told me that sometimes we can see even clearer when it's darkest," Babo said.

"We were watching a movie," Lucky Bat said.

"Use the dang flashlight, Babo!" Wage said, frustrated. They heard the sound of Babo digging through his pockets. He carried half his house around with him. There was something that sounded like a power drill in there, a whoopee cushion (or did he just fart?), and a car alarm remote. Finally, he switched on the light.

Ugly Dog was in front of the group, sniffing around the bottom of the tunnel. They could finally see ahead of them, or at least small glimpses of the tunnel's ceiling and walls.

"You smell anything?" Moxy asked.

"It's hard to say," Ugly Dog replied. "It would be easier if I had a nose...."

Before Moxy could respond, the group took a few steps forward, and the ground fell out from under them. Now they were falling through space, screaming and flailing and trying desperately to catch themselves. At some point, other dolls appeared, plummeting through the tunnel beside them. Then the tunnel split off, and each doll was directed into their own strange tube, where they slid through another corridor with bright lights, spiralling towards the ground.

As the slide looped around and around, it felt kind of like being on a roller coaster. (Moxy had never actually been on a roller coaster, but she had always imagined this was what it was like.)

"Ha-ha-ha, whoa! Yes!" she yelled, laughing. At the slide's end, Moxy shot out into a bright room. She landed in a pit of foam packing peanuts.

When Ugly Dog reached the bottom, he flew out of the slide with a strange blank-faced doll and was quickly buried in the peanuts, too. Wage and Lucky Bat were right behind him. It took them a moment to come to the surface.

"Yes, yes, yes!" Moxy yelled. She couldn't believe how scary, and then fun, and then even more fun that was. "Let's do it again!"

She tried to catch her breath, but the giant foam pit suddenly tipped to one side. Moxy, Wage, Babo, Lucky Bat, and Ugly Dog all spilled out onto the floor along with dozens of stiff, expressionless dolls.

Moxy brushed herself off and stared up at the giant gates in front of her. THE INSTITUTE OF PERFECTION was written above them in gold letters.

She wasn't sure where they were or what that meant, but at least they'd arrived somewhere. This was the first stop on the way to the Big World; it had to be....

CHAPTER 7

A laser light show started, projecting pictures and images on the walls. Then a voice came from all around them. "Welcome to the Institute of Perfection. Here you will train to be the best doll you can be. We will help you grow from Pretty to Perfect, but only after you successfully pass the great final challenge we call the Gauntlet. And now, please follow your guide-bots to the individualisation scanner. Enjoy your journey, and good luck."

Guide-bots? Individualisation scanner? Before Moxy and her friends could ask a single question, four robots appeared to guide them through the giant gates. Inside, other robots were separating the different dolls into lines. Each doll walked through the line and was scanned, and a voice announced what they were. The doll in front of Moxy was called "Susan," and the scanner told her she was "an engineer." But when it was Moxy's turn to be scanned, the system started going crazy.

"Alert!" the scanner blared. "Data does not compute!"

Smoke started coming out of it, then the machine twisted and fell onto the ground in a giant heap. All the lines came to a halt. Every single robot and doll turned towards Moxy and her friends, studying them for a good, long minute. Then the strange-looking dolls started shrieking and running in circles, desperately trying to put as much space between them and the UglyDolls as possible.

"Ahh...must be a customary greeting here," Lucky Bat said as one of the strange-looking dolls stepped over another one to get away from him. But when Lucky Bat returned the greeting with his own high-pitched wail, the doll fainted.

"Oh no," Babo said, frozen. "Is there something really scary behind us?"

Moxy glanced around, trying to figure out what

exactly had frightened the other dolls, but she wasn't sure. Maybe something about the scanner breaking had made them nervous. It couldn't have been her; she was sure of that.

Just then she spotted a giant television screen in the corner. "Guys! Look!" she said, unable to believe their luck. A slideshow was playing. It showed different dolls meeting their children for the first time. One video showed a girl opening a Christmas present and hugging her doll tightly. Another child ran around a birthday party, showing off his new doll to all his friends. There were children playing with their dolls in a park and children bringing their dolls to school.

Moxy's eyes filled with tears. This was her dream, played out a dozen different ways. She imagined what it would be like to be one of these lucky dolls, gifted to a child who would love and care for her forever.

A song started with the slideshow. It felt as if it were meant for just Moxy and no one else.

"*When it's time to meet your child, they will hug and hold you fast,*" the woman sang.

"As you bask in their affection,
That eternal, pure connection,
Thank the Institute of Perfection!
And it all begins…"

"Today," Moxy said, finishing the sentence.

She couldn't stop smiling. Her friends were right beside her, watching the video, too. They teared up as each child found their toy.

Ugly Dog turned to her in shock. After all this time, they were on their way to the Big World. They were going to find their children.

"Moxy…" he said, unable to believe it. "You were right."

CHAPTER 8

Ew!" someone yelled. "What are those?"

Moxy turned, wondering what they were talking about, and saw a group of three strange-looking dolls staring at them. They all looked the same, with thin arms and legs and humanlike features. They had long, shiny hair like humans, too.

"Is that one supposed to be a dog?" one of the humanlike dolls asked as she pointed at Ugly Dog. Her nose was scrunched in disgust.

"Are they *all* supposed to be dogs?" another one asked.

Moxy looked around her, at Wage, Babo, Lucky Bat and Ugly Dog. The humanlike dolls were talking about them. Why would they think they were all dogs?! She looked nothing like Ugly Dog!

"Lou is *not* going to like this," said the third humanlike doll.

Another tall, muscular doll strode over to the

humanlike girls. "Uh, excuse me, girls," he said. "Who's Lou?"

"No!" the first humanlike girl doll yelled. "*You* excuse me! *Who's Lou?*" she repeated, mocking him. "Were you born yesterday?"

Moxy had never heard of Lou, either, but she could tell that wasn't a good thing. Before the girl dolls could say anything else, the lights dimmed. Suddenly, the name LOU began flashing on the giant television screen and the crowd started chanting that name over and over again.

There was a long flight of stairs leading to a different part of the building, and a spotlight scanned all the way up it, finally landing on a handsome humanlike male doll. His hair was slicked back and he had big, burly muscles. As soon as the crowd saw him, they broke out into applause.

He sang, a microphone in his hand:

"If you want someone to love ya,
Babe, ya gotta look like me.

I mean, flawless, pure perfection, upper shelf.
And my first impression of ya,
As far as I can see,
Is you simply can't compete."

That doesn't seem very nice... Moxy thought.

He sang about how extraordinary his hair was.
He raved about his muscles and his profile. He
drew everyone's attention to his dance moves,
which he described as "hot", even though Moxy
and her friends couldn't feel any heat coming off
him when he twirled by. Honestly, if he had started
singing about his nose hairs, Moxy would not have
been surprised. He seemed to love every single
part of himself.

Then he went down the line and started
telling every doll what was wrong with them. He
called out double chins, blemishes, dolls that
were too short and dolls that were too thin. He
criticised yellow teeth, and he told a girl doll that
her nose started "right" but ended "all wrong."

The rest of the UglyDolls watched, horrified, as he sang about the other dolls' flaws. Apparently at this Institute, being "ugly" was not a good thing.

He sang:

> "Now, perhaps I've just upsetcha,
> But, people, let's get real.
> It's a most exclusive club that you want in.
> There's a price to pay, you betcha.
> Hey, you gotta look ideal."

Moxy could tell her friends didn't like Lou that much, but even he couldn't ruin her good mood. She was officially one step closer to the Big World and all the children in it. Maybe he was a bit… *harsh*, but being here had to be a good thing, right?

"*U-G-L-Y,*" Lou sang on. "*Face like that, why even try? U-G-L-Y! Bag that head like triple ply. U-G-L-Y! Sorry if that makes you cry; you're ugly!*"

Then he froze, pausing the entire song. He strode over to the UglyDolls and smiled his biggest, most dazzling smile. He leaned down and studied Moxy. She straightened up just a little taller. Then she pulled back her shoulders and smiled with all three of her teeth. Lou seemed to like that.

He sang:

> "I ain't seen nothing like you before!
> I mean, words fail me!
> I mean, I'm tongue-tied!
> I mean, I'm speechless, baby.
> Gotta tell you, girl, you're pretty..."

"I am?" Moxy said, her voice small.

Lou's smile faded. He stared at her, a puzzled look on his face. Then he shouted out the last line for everyone to hear. *"Pretty ugly!"*

Moxy just stood there, shocked. This Lou character, who seemed kind of important around here, thought she was ugly. She just kept staring ahead and smiling, but every time he opened his mouth she was worried about what he'd say next. How could he be so mean?

He continued, "*Imagine how you'd traumatise some unsuspecting youth. Why, it would be ugly! And that's the ugly truth.*"

When Lou's song ended, the UglyDolls weren't quite sure what to do. Every doll in the entire Institute was staring at them. Maybe some of them had a pimple or a crooked nose or freckles, but it was clear nothing was worse than being one of the UglyDolls. They were different.... They were the ugliest of the ugly, and here, that was not a compliment.

"I really do feel bad for you," Lou said, leaning in close. "But kids just don't want ugly, so it's probably better if you just go back where you belong."

Moxy felt as if her feet were glued to the ground. She tried hard not to cry.

Was Lou right? Did no one want her? Was she too... *ugly* to be loved?

CHAPTER 9

o one said a word. The crowd of dolls that
belonged – the Pretty Dolls – kept watching
the UglyDolls, waiting to see what they would
do next. Moxy felt as if the whole world had just
come crashing down on her.

"Come on, Moxy," Lucky Bat whispered. "Let's
just leave."

Babo picked up Ugly Dog and carried him out. The
rest of the UglyDolls followed, trying to ignore the
humanlike dolls who kept whispering and smirking.
It seemed as if everyone around them was talking
about how "hideous" and "revolting" they were.

"Bless their ugly little hearts," Lou said as they
walked past. "Such a shame."

Moxy glanced up, taking one last look at the
giant television screen. The slideshow was playing
again. In one slide, a child lifted a doll into her arms
and smiled. The little girl wiped away happy tears.

Moxy watched the little girl for a moment, and all her sadness lifted. There was a child out there for her somewhere. She could feel it in every inch of her plush-stuffed body.

That was it; she couldn't take it anymore. She marched up to Lou and got right in his perfectly chiselled face. "We're not going anywhere!" she said. "We may not look like you or act like you, but we can be pretty lovable.

"We're going to prove you wrong," Moxy continued, standing as tall as she could. Who was *Lou* to tell her she'd never find a child? "We're going to do the Gauntlet!"

Lou smiled, then threw his head back and laughed. The other Pretty Dolls laughed along with him, and the UglyDolls weren't sure why everyone was suddenly laughing, so they just starting laughing, too. It seemed like the right thing to do.

"Wait until Ox hears about this!" Babo said.

Lou stopped laughing and waved his hand

around until the others stopped, too. For a moment it seemed as if he knew Ox, but then his expression changed into something a bit more puzzled. "Ox? Who is Ox?" he asked.

"He happens to be the founder and mayor of our town," Lucky Bat said proudly.

"So…there's a whole town of Uglys," Lou said.

"What's it called? Uglyville?!" A Pretty Doll named Kitty laughed.

"Yes!" Moxy replied. "Have you been there?"

"Eww," the trio of girl dolls said. "You shouldn't be anywhere near the Gauntlet."

"Just because we're from Uglyville doesn't mean we can't compete in the Gauntlet," Moxy said. "Where does it say we can't? Show me the rule."

A robot rolled up beside Moxy and Lou, clutching a thick book in its metal hand. *Institute of Perfection Rule Book* was written on the cover. The robot flipped through the pages, but before it could find the rule, Lou grabbed the book and tossed it over his shoulder.

"Who knew this magical realm had a written set of rules?" Ugly Dog muttered.

"You know what?" Lou said. "Stay here."

Moxy glanced sideways at her friends. Was this a trick? "Really?"

"Yes!" Lou said. "What kind of benevolent leader would I be if I denied fellow dolls their chance in the Big World? Mandy," he called to another Pretty Doll. "I have a special task for you. Show them to their quarters. May I suggest the Supply Suite?"

Lou smiled a dazzling smile, and Moxy couldn't help feeling as if he'd reserved the brightest, most special place just for them.

"Sweet!" Babo said.

The UglyDolls followed Mandy down a long corridor, headed for their room.

CHAPTER 10

Mandy led them to a rickety supply shed. Cobwebs filled every crevice and corner, and musty boxes stuffed with old costumes, paint and crusty makeup were stacked to the ceiling. It looked as if no one had used the place for years.

"So here's your new home away from home," Mandy said, leading them inside. "I've never actually been here myself. It's so, uh...industrial chic."

The UglyDolls dashed inside, taking in all the little details. They looked under shelves and around a pile of dusty wigs. They'd never been somewhere so cool.

"What an emotional whirlwind; am I right?" Babo asked. "I wonder what our kids are like!"

"I bet mine loves music." Ugly Dog danced around the tiny shed. He kicked his heels together and did a quick little spin.

"Who cares? We're never gonna go," Wage said. "You heard the whole song, right? It was choreographed and everything."

Moxy tried to ignore Wage's comment. Sure, Lou's song was pretty vicious, but they were here, weren't they?

"Umm," Mandy went on. "Before I leave…I didn't get your names."

Moxy, Babo, Lucky Bat and Wage all introduced themselves to Mandy in rapid succession. Ugly Dog stepped forward last. "Folks call me Ugly Dog," he said.

"Because that's his name," Wage chimed in.

"But I prefer *Slick Dog*," Ugly Dog said.

"Which is *not* his name," Wage corrected.

Mandy just ignored them.

"So…are you guys really gonna try and train for the Big World?" she finally asked.

"You bet!" Moxy said, and the UglyDolls nodded in agreement. "And we're all gonna end up with our own special kid to love."

"You do know that Lou is gonna make that super hard for you, right?" Mandy asked.

Moxy didn't skip a beat. "Well, I say, bring it on, Lou!" she said cheerfully.

"I've never met anyone who could be so positive in the face of certain failure," Mandy said. She turned to go but bumped right into the wall. It knocked her off balance, and she tripped and fell to the ground. A pair of glasses slipped out of her pocket.

"Cool glasses!" Ugly Dog said, picking them up. "I always wanted some specs."

"*Ohh* yeah!" Moxy said, grabbing them and giving them a try, too. "I feel smarter already!"

"Excuse me!" Mandy reached out, trying to get them back. But the UglyDolls kept passing them around and trying them on.

"*Ohh....*" Babo loved the way he felt wearing them. As if he should be working in a library.

Mandy reached for the glasses again, but Lucky Bat had them, and then he passed them to Wage.

Mandy's face was turning redder, and she balled her hands into fists.

"Give them back right now!" she screamed.

The UglyDolls all went silent. They'd never seen someone so angry before.

"We're sorry..." Moxy said. The rest of the UglyDolls watched as Wage handed them back to Mandy.

"Don't tell anyone," Mandy said. "Especially Lou. Perfect Dolls have perfect eyesight, and I'm a Perfect Doll. Got it?"

The UglyDolls nodded.

"Good," Mandy said, an edge in her voice. Then she put on another big, perky smile and headed for the door. "Anyway, this was super-duper fun!" she called in a sing-songy tone. "I hope to chat with you again soon. Okay? *Byyyeee!*"

She turned and left, practically skipping past them as she went.

When Wage was certain she was gone, she turned to the others.

"Well, that was terrifying," she said.

The rest of the UglyDolls settled into their new home, trying to forget about Lou's song and Mandy's freak-out and why she was scared people would find out she wore glasses. They couldn't worry about that now.

Tomorrow was a big day, and they needed their Ugly sleep.

CHAPTER 11

The next morning, Lou paced in front of the dolls. "Today you begin your physical training," he said. "I know that seems stressful. Maybe a little scary. But remember, this is your purpose as a doll...and I would never let you fail! I've dedicated my entire life to making sure you go to the Big World. That's right," he went on. "I'm doing this for you! And you! And you!"

He started pointing at different dolls in the crowd.

"Me?" Nolan, a handsome male doll, asked.

"Yes, you!" Lou said cheerfully.

"Wait, so that whole 'you're ugly; you're trash' song...that was...because you love me?" Nolan asked.

"Yes! I love all of you!" Lou laughed. "And I will take you there!"

He pointed at the portal to the Big World, and an elaborate fireworks display went off.

The UglyDolls stood in the crowd, certain Lou was not talking to them.

"I know, I know," Lou went on. "It's awesome. *I'm* awesome. But first, your challenges!"

Lou pointed to the training field and set off another magnificent fireworks display. This one had three quick explosions of blue light. A final explosion at the end looked like a giant star.

"What's the fireworks budget here?" Ugly Dog said.

Three flags dropped down from the ceiling, labelling the three substances on the field.

"Baby food!" Lou called out. "Finger paint! Glue! The Big World is filled with unimaginable filth."

The Pretty Dolls stepped back in shock.

"What's wrong with glue?" Babo whispered to Lucky Bat. "You ever had it on a cracker?"

Lou got right into the Pretty Dolls' faces. "Do you want your clothes ruined by a tea party gone awry? Do you want to find yourself on the business end of a permanent marker? Today you're going to practice how to avoid stains, smudges and spills. Or as I like to call them...the *S*'s of messes."

Moxy knew she was supposed to be taking in all of Lou's Big World training tips, but she and her friends were too distracted by how fun the field looked. They couldn't stand it anymore....

They dove into the baby food and glue, throwing it at one another and laughing. Babo put a glob of baby food on Moxy's head and Moxy smeared some glue over Ugly Dog's back. They threw fistfuls of finger paint at one another. It didn't take long for Lou to notice their antics. The UglyDolls froze.

"Sorry, we were just having fun," Moxy said. "Was this part of the test?"

"Yes, it was," Lou said coldly. "And you passed! Enjoy the Big World!"

Lou gestured to two robots standing by a curtain. They pulled it back to reveal a large round opening.

"Thank you so much!" Moxy called out as she and her friends ran towards it. "You won't regret this, I promise."

The UglyDolls stepped through the door, and Lou slammed it behind them. They could hear him talking to the others through the glass window. "This, students, is what happens to dolls who get messy," he yelled, flicking a switch. "They get put through the wash!"

Water rushed in around Moxy's feet. Bubbles and soapy suds started filling the circular room. They were in something that Lou called a "washing machine," and he said that every time you were put in the washing machine you became less and less perfect until the child's parents threw you away. Thankfully, he stopped the machine before Moxy and her friends got tossed around too much.

"So if you want to pass these tests," Lou went on, "avoid messes. Stay out of the wash."

Moxy looked around at her friends, who were soaking wet and covered with bubbles. "He's right – we've gotta focus," she said. "No more messes."

No more having fun and laughing and starting fights with slimy, sticky substances that made hilarious smacking sounds when they hit your friends in the face. They'd have to be serious if they wanted to get to the Big World....

For the rest of the training, the UglyDolls tried the best they could to do everything just as Lou instructed them. There was a mechanical child that you had to hold on to even when it tried to throw you off, and Ugly Dog managed to stay on it for three whole minutes. Moxy sprinted on a treadmill without any trouble (she was used to running through town in excited fits), but then Lucky Bat accidentally got dipped in flour and had to go back to the washing machine.

The afternoon went on like that, with the UglyDolls having some big successes and some obvious failures. Moxy passed her psychological evaluation with flying colours. Lucky Bat carried a tray of teacups on his head but smashed into Wage because she wasn't watching where she was going. Ugly Dog got in a vicious fight with a mechanical dog, but at least he made it out with all his limbs.

At the end of the day, the UglyDolls had a particularly long run in the washing machine and then stood under the hair dryer until their fur was twice as puffy as normal. They sprawled out on the lawn, completely exhausted.

"My, my, I'm impressed..." Lou said as he strode past. "And yet...never mind."

"What?" Moxy asked.

"Far be it for me to discourage you," he said.

"Yeah, no, that's really hard to do." Moxy smiled.

"Of course it is," Lou replied. "But just between us, no matter how agile or unshakeable you may be, when you look up there at that perfectly Pretty doll and all the joy she comes with, do you honestly think your little band of sock puppets stands a chance here?"

It's another bright, shiny morning in Uglyville, where being weird and strange is normal - just ask the UglyDolls!

Moxy leaps out of bed and declares, "Today's the day!" She's sure she'll finally be chosen to go to the Big World and meet her human child.

Moxy's best friend is Ugly Dog. He helps Moxy deliver *The Daily Ugly* around Uglyville.

Lucky Bat is the wisest of the UglyDolls. Even though he always gives his friends great advice, he lacks confidence, especially when it comes to flying!

Wage is the best baker in Uglyville. She loves creating delicious treats for all her friends...

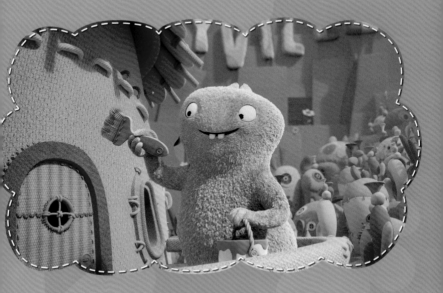

...and Babo loves eating Wage's treats! Babo is strong, sweet and an UglyDoll of few words.

The UglyDolls sing and dance every day to celebrate their friends, both old and new. They all love being Ugly!

Ugly Dog is an amazing rapper, and he *always* knows the perfect song to get the party going.

Ox is the mayor of Uglyville. He's a great leader *and* a great friend! He tries distracting Moxy from her hopes of meeting her child because he knows how long it's been since any UglyDoll was chosen to go to the the Big World.

Moxy is tired of waiting to be picked. She decides it's time to make her dreams come true - she'll go to the Big World and find her child herself!

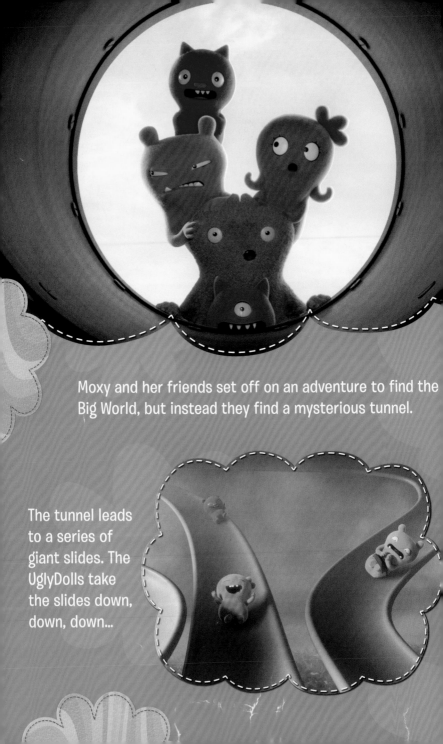

Moxy and her friends set off on an adventure to find the Big World, but instead they find a mysterious tunnel.

The tunnel leads to a series of giant slides. The UglyDolls take the slides down, down, down...

...all the way to a new world they never could have imagined.

The Institute of Perfection is filled with Perfect Dolls. They think being weird and strange is bad.

But no matter what the Perfect Dolls think, the UglyDolls know that being different makes them special!

Moxy looked at the giant screen in the centre of the arena. There was a clip of a little girl running through a field with her doll. The girl seemed thrilled to be with her, as if that doll was everything she'd ever wanted in a toy.

"Like I always say," Lou added, "Pretty makes perfect."

Lou walked off, leaving Moxy to think. He wasn't exactly *delicate* with his words. She started thinking about that Pretty Doll and all the mean things Lou had said, but then she realised that was it – that was just what they needed.

"We need an edge!" she said, turning to her friends. "And the way to do that is to make ourselves as Pretty as possible."

"Moxy, what are you talking about?" Babo asked.

Moxy stood and brushed off her nubby little knees.

"Everyone, come with me!" she cried.

CHAPTER 12

The storage shed was a mess. Old wigs, ripped clothes, broken jewellery and scraps of cloth covered every inch of the floor. The UglyDolls had opened every single box and bin in there, searching for new accessories. When they were finally done, Moxy stepped back to take in their new looks.

"I think it's an improvement," she said, studying herself in the cracked mirror on the wall. Wage, Babo, Lucky Bat and Ugly Dog were wearing ridiculously huge wigs. Moxy had on a yellow one that made her look as if she were from another century. Her cheeks were dusted with white powder and she wore a ratty tutu she'd found on the bottom shelf.

"Oh my doll…" Mandy said as she peeked into the room.

"We thought we'd give Pretty a try." Moxy shrugged.

"No, no, no." Mandy shook her head. "You need help right now – come on!"

She dragged them out of the shed and brought them down the hall to her own dressing room. Mandy had a whole cupboard filled with colourful, sparkly shoes and dresses. Her dressing table was covered with different gadgets and compacts to make her even more beautiful.

"Look, if I'm being honest," Mandy started, "I think you all looked great just the way you were. But if you're going to do this, can I do it for you? I've been doing makeovers since…as long as I can remember."

The UglyDolls all agreed. They could tell Mandy knew what she was doing. She always had on the coolest dresses and boots.

"*First we'll pluck a little here and tuck a little there,*" Mandy sang as she moved around the UglyDolls. She went to work, tweezing hairs and wiping off the crusty makeup they'd found in the shed. "*Then we'll cut a little loose and apply*

a little mousse to what seems to be… your
hair?"

Mandy moved around them, spraying some mousse on Moxy and plucking a stray hair from Ugly Dog's head. She passed out nail clippers, a comb and a nail file to the UglyDolls and then applied a big glob of lipstick to Moxy's lips.

"*So we'll try a little mask; it'll open up your pores,*" Mandy continued as she slathered some thick goo on Lucky Bat's face. Then she threw some cucumbers on the UglyDolls' eyes.

"*We're getting all dolled up!*" Mandy and the UglyDolls sang together.

Mandy ran a lint roller over Moxy's arms, Wage's legs and Babo's tongue, collecting bugs and twigs and cookie crumbs.

Mandy threw open the doors to her closet and the UglyDolls ran in, pulling out pleather trousers and feather boas and sparkly sequinned dresses. She helped them squeeze into the coolest, trendiest clothes she could find. When they each had decided on a great outfit, she pulled a sheet off the mirror and revealed their new looks.

"*We're getting all dolled up!*" they sang together. "*Feelin' fresh 'n' free! Because when you're all dolled up, people only see whatcha want them to see!*"

"Check us out!" Ugly Dog said, taking a spin in front of the mirror.

"We are Ugly-licious," Wage agreed.

"Wow," Moxy said, staring at her new reflection. She looked better than she ever thought possible. Every piece of fur was carefully combed into place. Her wig was divine, and her shoes actually matched her outfit – something she never realised was possible before.

"Thank you, Mandy," she said. Then the UglyDolls headed back into the arena, leaving Mandy alone.

When she was certain they were gone, Mandy studied her reflection in the mirror. She knew she was supposed to be a Pretty Doll, and she was supposed to be happy about that, but sometimes it felt like too much pressure. Why did they always have to listen to what Lou said? What did he know about being truly beautiful? Didn't it matter more that you were kind or smart or funny or happy...or all of those things?

Mandy sang to herself:

> "Look at me, all dolled up.
> Playing a part someone else agreed to.
> If I could choose who I could be..."

She paused, meeting her own gaze.

Now that she was making over her friends, telling them about prettiness, she'd never felt like a bigger fake. *"I'd choose a whole new me...."*

CHAPTER 13

Moxy and her friends stepped into the arena with their new and improved looks. Moxy was right – the makeovers gave them the confidence boost they needed. It was a real competitive edge.

"Just let me at that Gauntlet now," Babo said as the group walked right up to Lou and the trio of girl dolls, who called themselves the Spy Girls. "I am ready to *rummmble*."

"Well, what is this?" Lou asked.

"We're Pretty Dolls now!" Moxy announced.

"Hmm, you certainly are," Lou said.

"Why does he always say it with that tone?" Ugly Dog whispered to his friends.

"You're happy for us, then?" Moxy asked.

"*Sooo* happy." Lou smiled. "And yet so sad. You see, all your work has been for nothing."

"There it is," Ugly Dog muttered.

"No amount of make-up or fancy new clothes or manscaping can take away from the fact that deep down, you are *Ugly*Dolls. There's no changing that. UglyDolls can never pass the Gauntlet."

Lou shrugged, as if that were just the truth. Moxy looked sceptical.

"You don't believe me?" Lou asked. "I suspected as much. But maybe you'll believe *him*."

Lou stepped to the side, revealing Nolan. The tall, handsome doll seemed deeply confused. "Can – can you move?" Lou asked, trying to peer around him. Then he cleared his throat and started his menacing speech again. "But maybe you'll believe… *him*."

Nolan stepped to the side, revealing Ox.

The UglyDolls gasped.

"We kidnapped him!" Kitty, the meanest of the Spy Girls, shouted.

"I don't understand," Moxy said, though she was still excited to see him. "Ox, wait. You won't believe this – the Big World is real!"

"I know," Ox said, his voice serious.

"What?" Moxy looked around at the other UglyDolls, but they all seemed just as confused as she was.

Lou smiled. "Come on, Ox, why don't you relieve the poor creatures of their confusion. Why don't you start at the beginning?"

"Make it sound like a story!" Kitty yelled. The Spy Girls pulled out popcorn and settled in, their eyes wide with excitement.

"What's he talking about?" Moxy asked.

Ox was the one who always told her there was no Big World and she should stop dreaming about it. He thought she was silly for waking up every day determined to meet her child. And this whole time he knew that the Big World really did exist?! Why would he lie to her like that?

"It was a long time ago, before there was even an Uglyville..." Ox started. "When I was a brand-new doll. I don't know how it happened, but somehow I ended up here at the Institute.

Lou helped me become accepted among the Pretty Dolls. He made me better. We became best friends."

Moxy glanced sideways at Ugly Dog. Lou and Ox…best friends? How could that be?

"Then the big day came when I was to run the Gauntlet," Ox went on. "But I knew that would mean leaving my friend. So Lou and I decided we'd run the Gauntlet together. But something went wrong…" Ox closed his eyes, remembering what had happened that day. They'd got all the way to the end of the Gauntlet, but the door wouldn't open for them. The machine had said FAIL in big letters. It had wanted the robots to recycle him. "They all said it was my fault. Not even Lou could talk them out of it. That's when I learnt the truth about myself, about all the UglyDolls: We are rejects."

The UglyDolls stood there in shock.

"No…" Moxy said, tears filling her eyes.

"I managed to escape," Ox went on, "and block

the way to the Recycling Bin. Then I found our cove and built Uglyville, where reject dolls could live safe and free of anyone else's judgement."

Lou saw how upset the UglyDolls were at this news. "Oh, Moxy," he cooed. "This is what I've been trying to protect you from. But I realised you'd need to hear it from your oldest friend." He paused, letting this sink in. "You don't belong in the Big World. You don't belong anywhere...you're not supposed to exist."

I'm not supposed to exist? Moxy thought, and now the tears were coming fast. How could Ox lie to her all these years? How could he watch her get up every morning and chatter on about the Big World and her child when he knew for a fact she'd never get there? She'd told everyone she was going to the Big World one day – she'd even convinced them to come with her.

It was too much to take. Moxy turned away from the crowd, feeling an inch small. She couldn't think about the Big World for even a second longer.

"Moxy, Moxy!" Ox called after her. "I'm so sorry I lied."

"So there's no Big World for us?" She turned back to face him. "No kid waiting? I'm so sorry, everyone. This is all my fault. I should never have…"

Her voice started to break, and she couldn't stand there any more with everyone gawking at her. It was all too painful. She ran back to the gates and slipped out, leaving the Institute of Perfection forever.

CHAPTER 14

The sky above Uglyville was a cold, drab grey. Its colourful residents shuffled forward as if they were moving in slow motion. No one laughed or threw plush food or even smiled. It was as if all the life had been drained out of the place.

"Extra! Extra!" an UglyDoll with a newsboy hat called out. He waved a newspaper in the air. "People of Uglyville are revealled to be..."

"Rejects?" another UglyDoll said, reading the headline.

"Who'da thunk?" a bright-blue UglyDoll replied.

"I know...it's hard to thunk," Babo said. He stood outside the bakery, his shoulders slumped. He felt as if he'd been hit by a rickshaw.

After Moxy had left the Institute, Lou decided it was time for all the UglyDolls to return to their ugly little town and continue with their ugly little lives, far away from the perfection on the other side of the tunnel. Ox had wanted to keep the news about the Big World and the Institute a secret, but it spread faster than you could say, "Hideous rejects who will never be loved." Now it seemed as if everyone knew, and everyone was miserable for it.

"Yeah, it's time to wake up and smell the ugly." Wage put out a few bags of day-old pastries. Ever since she'd found out the truth, she'd stopped baking every day like she usually did. Sometimes it took great effort to make just one batch of decent cupcakes.

A small UglyDoll came over, and Wage handed her some stale doughnuts.

"Just the bag, please," the UglyDoll said.

Wage dumped the doughnuts onto the ground and set the paper bag on the UglyDoll's head. It had been like that all morning. No one actually wanted to eat any of her pastries any more – they just wanted something to hide their ugly faces.

A few blocks down, the UglyDoll who ran the party store was closing up shop. Lately, no one wanted to buy party hats or party poppers. No one in Uglyville wanted to *celebrate* anymore. He posted a sign on the door that read CLOSED DUE TO HOPELESSNESS.

Ugly Dog and Wedgehead rounded the corner and came across an UglyDoll who was slumped against a building.

"I wish I could say it wasn't so," Ugly Dog tried.

"Things will never be the same around here," Wedgehead agreed.

"Brother, can you spare a button?" the UglyDoll on the sidewalk asked. Ugly Dog threw him a button.

"Hard times," he said. "Hard, hard times."

If it was an ugly scene on the streets of Uglyville, it was even worse in the tiny crooked house a few blocks away. Moxy had barely left her bedroom since she'd come home. She was completely humiliated. All that singing and dancing and telling everyone about the Big World and her child! She was a reject, an unwanted toy who could never get through the Gauntlet!

She stared at all the drawings she'd made of herself with her child – a child who would never exist. There was one of them baking cookies and one of them at a tea party. There was one of them camping and another of them at the beach. There was a whole series of colourful, detailed pictures of them jumping on trampolines. (Moxy really, really loved trampolines.)

Now, after the Institute of Perfection, she didn't want to look at them any more. One by one, she ripped them off the wall and tore them to pieces. Then she slipped under her covers and went back to sleep.

CHAPTER 15

The next morning, the skies above Uglyville were still grey. The streets were mostly empty. Peggy the Pegacorn just barely made it to Moxy's window to wake her up.

"Hey," Peggy said flatly. "Wake up. Or don't. It doesn't matter."

Moxy stirred and sighed heavily. "I can't do this any more," she grumbled. But Peggy had already flown away. Moxy kicked her journal off the edge of her bed in frustration. It landed in the bin with a satisfying thud. Then she turned back over, not wanting to move.

"Did that make you feel better?" a familiar voice asked.

Moxy looked up to see Mandy standing in her doorway. Perfect, Pretty Mandy, from the

Institute, was in her room. But this time, she was wearing her glasses.

"What are you doing here?" Moxy asked.

"Moxy, you have to go back and complete the Gauntlet," Mandy tried.

What was Mandy even talking about? Had she not heard everything Ox said? There was no Big World at the end of the Gauntlet – not for her. No child would want a doll that was so... ugly.

"There's no point," Moxy said.

"That's where you're wrong." Mandy grabbed Moxy's journal out of the bin. "All your life, you knew the truth and you never stopped believing. And you were right! Everything you've done was right and *good*! Look how far you've got. You can't stop now."

"But Lou won't allow it..." Moxy said sadly.

"You can't stop now," Mandy repeated. "It's too important to all of us who are different – or even just feel less than perfect – that no one can get in the way of our true purpose." She walked Moxy over to her mirror and made her look at her reflection. "Moxy, this is bigger than you. Bigger than all of us. We haven't known each other very long, I know that, but one thing I'm sure of … you're not the kind of doll who'll let something break you."

Moxy frowned. She knew in her heart that Mandy was right; she never gave up. But how was she supposed to go back to the Institute? Could she really face Lou again after all the mean, terrible things he'd said to her?

Mandy sang to her friend:

> "There's always gonna be someone
> Messin' your head around,
> Watchin' you to see you break…"

She continued, "*Don'tcha let them in your head – never mind the lies they spread.*"

They sang together:

"Get up on your feet instead,
And then show 'em who you are.
Show 'em that you're strong.
Show 'em they've been seeing you all wrong.
Open up their minds,
Throw away the key,
Tell 'em that you are,
And you'll always be,
Unbreakable..."

CHAPTER 16

"Great song, guys!" a cheerful voice said once they'd finished.

Moxy and Mandy turned to see Kitty and the other two Spy Girls, Lydia and Tuesday, standing in the centre of Moxy's room. They'd been watching the whole time. Kitty was holding a huge burlap sack.

Before Mandy and Moxy could respond, the Spy Girls grabbed them and shoved them inside the sack. Everything was dark. Moxy could feel them bumping down the stairs and being carried through the streets. They tried to scream, but no one could hear them.

"Let us out!" Moxy yelled.

"No way – Lou's orders," Tuesday grumbled.

"Do you always do what Lou tells you?" Mandy asked.

"Yeah. Obvi," Tuesday said through the sack.

Moxy and Mandy bumped and banged around inside the bag. It felt as if the Spy Girls were dragging them over rocks, up and down a hundred staircases and through a giant sandpit. When the girls finally dropped the sack, Moxy and Mandy climbed out of the bag and into a dark passage. They could barely see the two feet in front of their faces.

"Lou?" Tuesday said.

"You didn't think I was going to miss all the fun, did you?" Lou asked.

Kitty looked confused. "You did miss the whole *climbing down, kidnapping, dragging, climbing back up and being tired* part."

"I see you brought Mandy, too; how delightful," Lou said.

"I've come up with a plan." Lou moved to the side, revealling a hole in the ground. It was the pipe that led to the Recycling Bin, where dolls were destroyed. Moxy's stomach twisted in a knot. "Do you know how hard I've worked?" he asked Moxy. "Those Pretty Dolls...they're mine. They hang on my every word. Do what I say. Think what I think. Cut my cuticles! Brush my silky hair at night! And if you think I'm going to let you take that away from me...you're as empty-headed as the rest of them."

Lou looked over at Mandy. He grabbed her glasses off her face and threw them on the floor, stomping them with his expensive loafer. "You're both ugly," he said to Moxy and Mandy. "And ugly things belong in Recycling."

"You can't do this!" Mandy cried as Lou grabbed her arm.

"All dolls end up where they're supposed to be," he said, and he pushed Mandy down the pipe. He threw Moxy down after her. "But don't worry – we'll see each other again soon. You'll be brand-new. You'll be...Perfect."

Mandy and Moxy screamed as they fell down the pipe. They tried to grab on to the walls, but they were too slippery. They kept falling, faster and faster, moving closer and closer to their doom.

CHAPTER 17

Moxy couldn't tell how long they'd been in there. The long pipe ended in a metal room. Pieces of broken toys littered the floor. She jumped up, trying to reach a trapdoor above them, but it was just out of reach.

"Moxy, give it up," Mandy said sadly. "We already tried."

All of a sudden, a light above them flashed red. A whirring sound filled the air, as if some machinery deep inside the Recycling Bin were waking up. Moxy and Mandy grabbed hold of each other.

When they turned around, two red eyes glowed before them. A huge, mashing mouth appeared below the eyes, its terrible metal teeth chomping up and down. A conveyor belt under them turned on, and they started slowly moving towards the mouth. They were about to be smashed and mashed and recycled.

They ran as fast as they could in the opposite direction, trying to get away from the compactor. But there was so much debris and broken toys on the conveyor belt that they kept tripping. Moxy got pinned under a piece of plastic.

"*Ahhh!*" Moxy squeezed her eyes shut, worried this was the end.

"Moxy!" a familiar voice shouted.

Moxy looked up to see Ox, Lucky Bat, Wage, Ugly Dog and Babo drop in from the trapdoor in the ceiling. Wage ran over and kicked off the piece of plastic that had pinned Moxy down.

"Ready, Wage?" Babo asked, seeing that they were all finally free. "Now!"

Everyone joined hands in one straight line. Then Babo and Wage jumped up and wedged their feet against the wall so that all their friends were jammed together, floating just above the moving conveyor belt. It was a good fix, but they wouldn't be able to stay like that forever.

Lucky Bat stared at the trapdoor above them. He flapped his wings as hard as he could, trying to fly through it, but it was no use. "Oh, forget it," he mumbled.

"Woulda been super dramatic," Babo agreed. He whistled, and a few UglyDolls appeared at the trapdoor. They were holding on to one another's hands and legs, forming a doll chain that reached all the way down to the bottom of the pipe. Wedgehead led the group. She swung the chain back and forth, and the UglyDolls grabbed on. But just as they were able to link up with Moxy and the others, one side of it slipped. The back of the chain landed on the conveyor belt.

Everyone managed to hang on except Babo. He was now running as fast as he could up the conveyor belt, but with each passing second, he got closer to the horrible chomping jaws of the machine. He threw every item he could find into it. He pulled screwdrivers from his pocket, extra buttons, lightbulbs and a toaster. But nothing satisfied the Recycling machine. It ate all of them and still was hungry for Babo.

Moxy was the closest to him. She reached out, but he was always a tiny bit beyond her grasp. Just then she got an idea. She leaned over and offered her head to Babo. The tiny flower-shaped pouf on top of it was just the extra length they needed. He grabbed on, and the rest of the dolls started pulling them forward.

"Pull!" Wedgehead ordered, and they got a little further from the machine.

"Pull!" Tray, another UglyDoll, called out.

Inch by inch, they were pulled all the way up the pipe and out into the open air. Willard was at the end of the doll chain, and he kept running forward until every single doll was safe. When Moxy got onto solid ground, it took her a minute to realise they were back in Uglyville. There was an entrance to the pipe not far from the centre of town.

Every resident of Uglyville was either in the doll

chain or standing in the crowd, cheering them on. They'd all come out to help save her.

"I'm lucky you got that thing on your head, whatever it is," Babo said to Moxy. He was still out of breath from all that running.

Moxy touched her head thing. She'd always thought it was a weird growth, but now she saw it as a special tool. Maybe it was her superpower.

"We're all here for you, Moxy," Ox said.

"Oh my gosh," Moxy said, realising he wasn't exaggerating. "You're all here. Ice-Bat's here, and Wedgehead. Jeero and Big Toe. Trunko, Fea Bea, Winkolina–"

"No need to list the whole town," interrupted Wage. "We're kind of in a rush."

"Fair enough!" Moxy agreed. She couldn't stop smiling. No matter how scary it had been to be in the Recycling Bin with Mandy, she knew now that no one could stop her, especially not a nasty Perfect Doll like Lou.

"I'm done feeling like I don't belong," she said.

"I'm not a reject. None of us are. And we're going to run that Gauntlet! We are unbreakable!"

The crowd erupted into cheers.

Moxy laughed, feeling better than she had in weeks. She couldn't wait to see Lou's face when she raced across the finish line....

CHAPTER 18

The arena was packed with dolls. There were hundreds of them, eating popcorn and drinking sodas and wondering who would get through the Gauntlet this year. High above, two announcer robots provided commentary for the event. It wasn't long before the lights dimmed and a giant dollhouse rose out of the arena floor. This was the elaborate maze every doll would have to make it through.

Lou walked into the single spotlight on the arena floor. "Are you ready for the Gauntlet?" he yelled into the crowd. Everyone screamed and cheered.

"I said..." Lou cupped a hand over his ear as if he couldn't hear them. "Are you ready?!"

"Yes!" a small voice yelled. "Excuse me, sorry. Coming through."

"Mandy?" Lou asked, trying to hide the surprise

in his voice. Mandy charged into the arena. All the Uglyville residents came in behind her and found seats.

"Hmmm…it appears something is amiss in our schedulling," Dirkbot, one of the announcers, said.

Moxy and her friends weren't far behind the big crowd. She strode into the arena alongside Ox, Wage, Babo, Ugly Dog and Lucky Bat, their heads held high.

"Hello, old friend!" Ox called out to Lou.

"Oh, this is rich," Lou muttered. "This is really rich. You can't possibly think you'll pass."

"Maybe we will; maybe we won't," Moxy said proudly. "But every doll in this stadium is going to see us try!"

Mandy stepped forward, a smirk on her lips. "Oh, Lou, you should totally compete in the Gauntlet and show them how it's done!" Mandy turned to the crowd and led them in a cheer. "Lou, Lou, Lou, Lou!"

Soon the entire arena was chanting Lou's name.

They all wanted him to compete. How could he possibly say no?

"*Aaah*, why not? Right?" Lou finally agreed. Then he turned to Mandy and narrowed his eyes. "It really is a shame, Mandy. You showed such promise."

"You know what, Lou? When I first got here, I thought you were perfect. I couldn't find a single thing wrong with you," she said. Then she pulled her old pair of glasses out of her pocket and put them on. "But I can see a lot better now."

Then Mandy turned around and took the elevator to the top of the dollhouse with Moxy and the rest of the UglyDolls. It was jam-packed with the other Pretty Dolls who were competing. The announcer bots explained what would happen next.

"Now, as you all know," Dirkbot said, "the Gauntlet is designed to simulate real-world obstacles."

"The participants must make it through the doggie door and cross the finish line in the regulation four minutes," the other announcer bot, Seemabot, said.

Mandy, Moxy and the other UglyDolls stood at the lift doors. They took a deep breath. This was it. They'd finally made it to the Gauntlet. Lou was packed into the lift beside them, and he still seemed furious about Mandy's comment. They all stood there waiting for the starting bell in total silence.

Bing! The bell sounded, and then they were off. The UglyDolls rushed through the entry hall of the dollhouse, jumping on furniture and bouncing off the walls. They spotted the staircase up ahead and ran towards it, but a massive robotic dog jumped out at them, blocking their way down. Moxy and her friends scattered, and the dog grabbed Nolan, the handsome doll, in its jaws. It shook him violently.

Tuesday wanted to save him, but Lou wasn't having it.

"He's a lost cause!" Lou yelled out. "He's gone forever!"

Nolan clutched the door frame just inches from Lou and reached out to him. "I'm over here!" Nolan yelled, right in Lou's face. "You could grab my hand!"

Lou just watched as the robotic dog dragged him away.

"There's nothing we could have done," Lou declared, shaking his head. Then he took off, running deeper into the Gauntlet.

As the UglyDolls found their way back to the stairs, the robotic pooch dropped Nolan and turned its eyes on Ugly Dog.

"You call that a *dog*?" Ugly Dog laughed. "It's all right, guys. *Slick Dog*'s got this."

He started dancing around, breaking out his most impressive moves. He spun and shoulder rolled and hip gyrated until his robotic rival was cheering him on. It was just the distraction the UglyDolls needed. They jumped atop Babo's big belly and slid down the staircase banister together.

"I can't believe that actually worked!" Babo laughed when they all landed safely at the bottom of the stairs.

The Pretty Dolls had run down the stairs and been attacked by a vacuum cleaner that was hiding in a side cupboard. It gave the UglyDolls a slight advantage as they made their way into the laundry room. Steam cleaners blasted at them, an ironing board crashed down from above, and the iron went swinging by its cord, nearly knocking them all over. But Lou was the real problem. He had jumped on top of the washing machine and now was throwing toilet paper rolls at them. When that didn't slow them down, he poured bleach all over the floor. Moxy and her friends jumped onto sponges and wedges of toilet paper and skidded through the mess to the other side.

Mandy had lost the rest of the UglyDolls in the chaos of the dollhouse. She ran through the laundry room. Out of the corner of her eye, Mandy spotted Lou with a giant box of powdered soap.

He was pushing it towards the edge of the washing machine, about to dump it right on Moxy's head.

"*Moooooxy!*" Mandy yelled. She dove forward, trying to stop Lou, but then the box of powdered soap fell on her instead. Moxy stopped to help, but Mandy urged her to leave. "Go, Moxy! Keep going!"

Moxy turned to the clock. Mandy was right – Moxy couldn't stay and help her *and* make it to the doggie door in time. She had to choose. Wage and Lucky Bat rushed to Mandy's side, and so Moxy kept going, sprinting through the obstacle course with the others.

Moxy and Ox raced through the living room. A toy bulldozer charged at them. It took them a second to realise Lou was at the controls, slamming its massive arm down around them, trying to squash them like bugs. Then, in one quick motion, the bulldozer scooped up Moxy and Ox. They were stuck – there was no way out now.

"*Ahhh!*" Moxy screamed as it spun them around and around. "*Oooox!*"

CHAPTER 19

Ox used his long ears to move Moxy into the tiny driver's seat. Moxy pounded some of the buttons on the dashboard, trying to override the controls Lou had been using. Soon she was steering the bulldozer herself. She drove away from the dryer and slammed her foot on the gas, speeding around different obstacles.

Moxy could see the finish line at the bottom of the second staircase. She made a sharp turn and the bulldozer went flying down the stairs. Moxy and Ox held on tight as it careened over Lou's head. "*Wooo-hooo!*" they cheered.

Behind them, a life-size robot baby grabbed Lou and shook him in his fist. Moxy and Ox were certain they were in the clear, but then the robot baby reached for the bulldozer. He picked it up and hurled it in the other direction. They both fell from the front seats and skidded out over the floor. Ox landed so hard, his head was spinning. He tried to get up, but his legs were pinned under the toy bulldozer.

"My head...feels..." Ox mumbled. "Not good."

Moxy leaned in to help him, and she felt something squeeze her entire body. She turned around and saw that the robot baby had grabbed her in his giant hand. He shook Moxy in one fist and Lou in the other. He kept screaming, "*Goo goo gah gah*," and a bunch of other baby noises.

Far below them, all the Pretty Dolls and UglyDolls were already at the doggie door. They pushed on it and tried to jam their fingers under it to lift it up, but they couldn't figure out how to get it to open. One Pretty Doll rammed into it with a toy block, but that didn't work, either.

Then Ugly Dog came down the stairs, riding his new robot dog. He was headed directly for the doggie door. "Is it okay for a pet to have his own pet?" he yelled to no one in particular.

"Yes!" Ox cheered from under the bulldozer.

All it took was a tiny nudge from the giant robot dog, and the doggie door opened. All the UglyDolls rushed through it. This enraged Lou, who was still being held hostage by the robot baby.

"Unhand me, you annoying little hazard!" Lou shouted. "Let go now!"

He started kicking and punching the baby until he landed a particularly good kick right on the baby's nose. The robot baby's face turned bright red and he let out a loud, sorrowful wail. Then he threw Moxy over one shoulder and Lou over the other. Moxy landed on the floor with a *thud*.

"I've never seen anything like this!" Seemabot, one of the announcer robots, said. "They just might make it!"

The time was ticking down. There were only thirty seconds left. The baby had thrown Lou into a tall toy box that was hard to get out of, and Moxy saw her last chance. She jumped up and sprinted as fast as she could to the doggie door.

"Unprecedented!" Dirkbot cried. "These UglyDolls are about to make history!"

The crowd cheered. Every doll in the arena was on their feet, their arms raised in the air. They were screaming and clapping for Moxy and her friends.

Moxy stared at the doggie door in front of her. She was so close…she was going to make it after all. She just had a few more feet to go.…

That's when she heard it. Somewhere behind her, the robot baby had started crying. She looked up into his face, which was red and streaked with tears. He looked so sad and so alone. He was crying much harder than before, his whole body shaking with the effort.

Moxy couldn't just leave the baby there. She wouldn't. Instead, she did the unthinkable – she stopped running for the finish line.

Lou saw his opportunity and climbed out of the toy box. He raced past her, nearly knocking her down as he sprinted for the doggie door. But Moxy still couldn't leave the baby. Instead, she walked towards him. She climbed up the baby's belly and into his arms.

"It's okay," she cooed. She stared into the baby's big eyes. He looked terrified, and his nose was still red from where Lou had kicked him. "Don't cry. You'll be okay."

The baby stared back. Just being with Moxy seemed to calm him down. Moxy wrapped her tiny arms around him as best she could, and the baby hugged her back, squeezing her close to his chest.

Mandy and the rest of the UglyDolls were already past the doggie door, just steps away from the finish line. They would just have to go a little further if they wanted to win. But they all turned back and watched as Moxy comforted the baby.

The child seemed happier now, snuggling up against Moxy. He rocked her in his arms. How could the UglyDolls cross the finish line without their friend? They knew there were only seconds left on the clock and they would lose if they didn't run across right then, but they just couldn't leave her.

Lou darted past them and ran across the line. He raised his arms in triumph. But when he looked up at the giant monitor, it wasn't focused on him. It was playing the live footage of Moxy hugging the robot baby. The whole arena had gone silent, and everyone was watching them, moved by how gentle and sweet she was being.

One by one, Mandy and the rest of the UglyDolls joined her. They surrounded the baby in a giant group hug, Ox's long ears wrapped around his friends. There were only a few seconds left on the clock, but none of them cared.

They wouldn't make it, and that was okay. They all still had one another.

CHAPTER 20

"Sorry we didn't pass," Moxy said, looking up at her friends. They were all still snuggled up in the baby's arms. She'd wanted to go through the Gauntlet more than anyone, but it didn't matter now.

Just then one whole side of the dollhouse slid back, revealing the crowded arena. Every single doll was on their feet, cheering for Moxy and her friends. The scoreboard at the top of the arena had all their names listed, and each UglyDoll's name lit up with PASS beside it.

"You did it, Moxy!" Mandy smiled.

Moxy hugged the baby even tighter. The child was smiling and laughing now.

Three bots rolled into the dollhouse. "You have fulfilled a doll's true purpose," they said, referring to how Moxy had helped the child. That was way more important than her crossing any finish line. "New data received. Run celebration protocol."

Confetti exploded out of the robots' heads. The crowd starting dancing and cheering even louder. Lou was the only one in the entire stadium who seemed upset. He tried to charge the UglyDolls, but the robot dog swatted him back. Then his name lit up on the scoreboard with FAIL next to it.

"Look!" Nolan shouted. He was a bit mangled from his encounter with the robot dog, but he could still stand. He pointed towards the scoreboard and Lou's big FAIL. Everyone in the arena turned to stare.

Lou looked around. He was nervous at first, but then his expression changed. He narrowed his eyes at the UglyDolls and laughed maniacally.

"Well, I guess the cat's out of the bag!" he snarled.

"Lou, what do you mean?" Tuesday asked. "How could you fail?"

"You still don't get it," Lou grumbled. "Of course I

failed!" He threw his head back and stared up into the sky, shouting into the abyss, "*I'm a prototype!*"

The whole arena was quiet. "What?" Mandy finally said.

"*Prototype*'s, like, a good thing, right?" Tuesday asked.

"You thought I stuck around this place because I cared so much about you mindless sycophants?" Lou laughed.

"*Sycophant*'s, like, a good thing, right?" Tuesday asked again.

"Ugh. No, you imbecile," Kitty snapped. A sycophant was someone who worshipped someone else. Who did whatever they were told to do.

"Is *imbecile* a good thing?" Tuesday whispered.

"My gut says...yes," Babo replied.

"I'm the model," Lou explained as he paced. "The mould! Sent by the factory to help guide you through. Sounds amazing, right?"

"Uh..." Nolan tried. "Right?"

"Wrong!" Lou yelled in his face. "Prototypes are not meant for public consumption. I was never allowed to go to the Big World!" He turned and pointed a finger at Ox. "But *you* could. Let's see how you feel when you're trapped in this place forever. Just like me."

Lou ran back into the dollhouse to a basket of wool and knitting needles. He grabbed a knitting needle and then pushed a button on the wall, which caused the whole dollhouse to slowly lower into the ground. The giant baby scooped up all the UglyDolls and tossed them out of the house, just before it disappeared from view.

The horrified crowd looked on as Lou took the elevator to the dollhouse roof. The UglyDolls, Mandy, the Pretty Dolls and the Spy Girls charged him at once. He was heading straight towards the portal. The knitting needle was aimed directly at it.

"Come on!" Kitty yelled to the others as they all raced to beat him there.

Ox flipped over and used his long ears as legs

so he could run twice as fast. He got to the portal door right as Lou did. He stretched out his ears, trying to stop Lou from jabbing the knitting needle into the portal doors.

"What happened to you?" Ox asked sadly. "We were like brothers."

Lou slipped from his grasp and spun around. The two started sparring. Lou came at Ox again and again, trying to get away from him so he could push through the portal.

"You, a reject, were going to leave me like the others," Lou said. "Ever wonder why the Pretty Dolls turned on you?"

"You sabotaged me and tried to have me recycled!" Ox yelled. Both his ears were fighting off Lou. They grabbed Lou for a brief moment and flung him sideways, but then the two were fighting again.

"You wanted to leave so badly? I sent you right where you belong!" Lou spun around and stabbed the portal door with the knitting needle. It cracked just the tiniest bit. Soon he'd break through to the other side. "The only thing I did wrong was not waiting to make sure you were recycled."

Lou jabbed at the portal once more, and it shattered, sending both Ox and Lou flying. The UglyDolls charged forward and tried to help their friend. Lou and Ox were still so far away, though.

"I need a boost!" Lucky Bat said to Babo. If they didn't stop Lou right now, he'd make it to the other side.

Babo searched through his pockets. "I got nothing."

"We've got each other," Lucky Bat said. The UglyDolls surrounded Lucky Bat and formed a makeshift slingshot with their soft, plush bodies. They ran back and then launched Lucky Bat into the air. With newfound confidence, he spread his wings and flew towards the portal doors, heroically landing right in front of Lou to block his path.

Lucky Bat grabbed the knitting needle from Lou and hit him over the head with it.

He hit him again, this time in his side, and Lou went flying.

"*Gaaaaaahhhhh!*" Lou screamed.

Babo and Wage caught Lou and grabbed his hands and feet. They swung him back and forth, back and forth. Then they tossed him over to Ugly Dog, who was still riding the robot canine. The giant mechanical dog caught Lou in his metal jaws and clamped them shut.

"Good dog!" Moxy cheered. Lou was trapped behind the robot dog's teeth, which formed a metal cage. They finally had him right where they wanted him.

CHAPTER 21

"Girls! Girls!" Lou shouted to the Spy Girls from inside the dog's mouth. "Are you gonna let them take over after everything I've done for you?"

Mandy and the UglyDolls turned to Kitty, sure this was it. This was the moment where she made a big speech and turned on them and set Lou free. But instead she just looked to Moxy. "So, where should we put him, boss?" she asked.

"Hmmm…" Moxy smiled. "I haven't decided. Any suggestions?"

"Recycle him!" a doll in the back of the group called out.

"Shred the liar!" a particularly enraged Pretty Doll shouted.

"Let the dog have him…" Another Pretty Doll smiled mischievously.

Moxy glanced around, a little taken aback. She

had no idea these Pretty Dolls were hiding so much rage. *Shred the liar?! Let the dog have him?!*

"No, please," Lou begged from inside the dog's mouth. "Please, I know I'm not Perfect, but I deserve a second chance. Look into your heart!"

"Uh, I have an idea…" Babo said. He and Nolan had been planning something in the back of the crowd. Nolan was now standing in front of a giant curtain. He tugged at a rope, and the curtain fell, revealing… the washing machine.

"*Noool*" Lou screamed louder than he ever had before.

The robot dog ran towards it with Lou in his mouth. He tossed Lou into the wash, and the "Perfect" Doll spun around and around, suds hitting against the glass window. It felt like a victory, at least for a fleeting moment, but then Wedgehead noticed what was happening.

"Hey, guys…" she said. "Something's not right with the portal."

The crowd turned back to the shattered glass

doors. The light beyond it glowed brightly one last time and then faded into darkness. The rest of the glass fell to the ground in thousands of tiny pieces.

Moxy walked up the steps to the portal and stared into it. There was nothing beyond it now. No beautiful glowing light. No way to the Big World and all the loving children there. How would she find her child now?

"*There's a child for every doll...*" she sang sadly. "*But I guess that's not quite true. There won't be one for me now...*" She turned to her friends and pointed to Lucky Bat, Ugly Dog and Mandy. "*Or for you... or you... or you.*"

"*I can't believe it's over,*" Ox added, singing along. "*And Lou will get his way.*"

"*Even dreamers have to wake up,*" Lucky Bat chimed in. "*Guess today will be the...*"

Lucky Bat couldn't finish his thought. All the UglyDolls were overcome with sadness. They realised then that even if they hadn't sung every morning the way Moxy had or talked about finding their child, it had always been a hope. Who were they if they couldn't dream?

Moxy stared at her reflection in a cracked pane of glass. She couldn't believe this was really how it would end. Then she smiled at herself, wondering if maybe there *was* something she could do....
Maybe there *was* another way. She'd come this far; it wasn't like her to just give up now.

"*Show 'em who you are...*" she sang, channelling all her hopes and dreams into the dark portal. She reached out and touched the broken doors. There was just the faintest glow around her stubby fingers. She could feel something incredible happening.

"*Show 'em that you're strong...*" Mandy sang, stepping up beside her. Mandy reached out, too, focusing all her energy on the portal. She glanced over to Moxy. As soon as their eyes met, their powers doubled, and all the optimism and bravery they ever felt came rushing out of them. The portal glowed brighter.

"*Show 'em that you know where you belong,*" they sang together.

"*Open every door...*" Ox joined in, raising his hand to the portal.

"*Own your own destiny...*" Lucky Bat added.

The portal glowed even brighter, and Moxy could feel their love and hope transforming it. The Pretty Dolls and Spy Girls rushed forward to join the UglyDolls. Soon everyone had a hand on the broken doors, and they were all smiling as the light grew brighter and brighter.

"*Look down deep in your heart and believe in the you that you see,*" Moxy sang.

"*Then become who you are and you'll set yourself free,*" Mandy joined Moxy, and they sang together.

The dolls all stared straight ahead into the portal as it roared back to life. The glow kept getting brighter as they sang, until everything in front of them was a beautiful blinding white. It was so incredible, they could barely speak.

Moxy smiled, and the tears welled in her buggy little eyes. She'd done this. She'd made this happen; she'd brought back hope to all of Uglyville.

The future looked... *bright*.

CHAPTER 22

The crowd huddled around Ox. He stood in front of the mountainside with the giant sunflower. New slides and roller coasters came out of the mountain now, connecting the Institute of Perfection with Uglyville. Ox held scissors in the air, about to cut a long ribbon that stretched out in front of them.

"As your mayor," he called out, "I'm proud to announce the permanent merger of Uglyville and the Institute of Perfection!"

Ox cut the ribbon in half, and it fell to the ground. The crowd cheered. In an instant, dozens of Pretty Dolls came down the slides and roller coasters, screaming with joy as they finally landed in Uglyville.

After they restored the portal, they'd spent days connecting the two cities. They'd tried to think of the most fun, most exciting ways to join them together. UglyDolls climbed into roller-coaster cars and were shot right to the top of the mountain. They screamed and cheered, their eyes wide with delight.

"Welcome one and welcome all to Uglyville and the Institute of Perfection!" Peggy the Pegacorn shouted. She flew through the air, dipping and diving among the new citizens.

Moxy was already passing out a newsletter that announced the joining of the two towns. Everywhere she turned, Pretty Dolls and UglyDolls were coming together in a real way. Everyone was laughing and smiling. Lucky Bat flew over the crowd and dropped confetti and glitter on them. Babo and the Spy Girls painted the dollhouse barracks in bright, crazy colours. Mandy helped different Pretty Dolls and UglyDolls try on new looks.

Ox and Wage took the roller coaster up to the Institute of Perfection and the portal so they could usher each doll through to the other side. Now that the portal was restored, every doll would be able to find their child. They'd finally become a birthday present or a Christmas present or a Just Because present. They'd finally see the look of delight and surprise as their child opened the box. They'd finally feel warmth and love as their child snuggled them in their arms.

"*Now the portal, permanently opened wide,*" Ox sang as the first dolls stepped through. "*You can go be with your child on the other side.*"

"*You may come back,*" Wage whispered. "*Once the kid hits the sack.*"

Just then Ugly Dog burst in, bringing a long, twisty conga line of dolls with him. They were all dancing and laughing and getting ready to meet their children. In seconds, the area around the portal turned into a huge party.

Ugly Dog sang as he danced, "*This old dog has learned a new trick – being Ugly is better than slick.*"

"*See, Ugly is different,*" the Spy Girls sang together. "*Ugly's unique. It's keeping it real when you feel like a freak. So face it, embrace it and follow your bliss."*

"*It doesn't get better than this!*" Ugly Dog added.

Wage and Legs the octopus came in with heaping plates of food. They had every kind of dumpling, doughnut and cake imaginable. They passed the plates out to the dolls as they danced and spun around in the wild party outside the portal. It wasn't long before Moxy joined in and a great chorus swelled up around them.

"*Yes, it's a mixed-up life in our inside-out world,*" Moxy sang, leading her friends, old and new. It was hard to keep singing when she was smiling and laughing so much. She couldn't remember ever being so happy.

> "It's amazing, you bet,
> But there's something much better—
> So amazing, and yet,
> It gets even much better.
> There's one thing that's better...."

They looked at the portal, restored in all its glory. It was glowing with a beautiful white energy. Finally the UglyDolls in Uglyville knew that Moxy had been right. There was something on the other side of Uglyville waiting for all of them. Better than anything they could have ever imagined or hoped for. And it didn't matter what they looked like, or if they had a missing eye or four sharp fangs – they would all be loved.

Moxy climbed the stairs towards the portal as the rest of the UglyDolls looked on.

Ox smiled. "Well, Moxy," he said. "Today's the day."

"I never doubted you, girl," Wage added. "Not for one minute. Well, okay, maybe for, like, one minute, or maybe, like, five to ten – time here is so funky. I mean, how long did this take us – what is this? A day, a month? What, eighty-three minutes? This is all so confusing." Wage stared off, deep in thought. It took her a moment to realise Moxy was still staring at her. "But look, you better come back to visit, you hear me?"

"Of course I'm coming back. Uglyville is my home," Moxy said. Then she turned to Lucky Bat. "You were right the whole time...we found our own truth."

She smiled at her friends one last time, then turned back to the glowing portal. The light was so bright, she couldn't see anything beyond it. She took one step forward, then another, until...

Suddenly Moxy was in another room. Only it wasn't a room; it was a box. Someone was opening the top of it. Huge hands lifted her out and put a ribbon on her head. The tag had HAPPY BIRTHDAY, MAIZY printed on it in block letters. Then the person carried her into a huge bedroom lit only by a soft night light.

"*Shhhhh...*" one of the parents said. "Don't wake her up. She's going to love it!"

They placed Moxy down on the floor beside a few wrapped boxes. Other toys were strewn about. Moxy didn't want to get mixed up with the riffraff – stray blocks and odd puzzle pieces – so as soon as she was sure the parents were gone, she scrambled up onto the bed. She stepped over a diary, accidentally knocking it to the floor. It landed with a thud.

The little girl rolled over. Then she sat up and rubbed her eyes. She looked around, trying to figure out where the sound had come from. There, sitting on the edge of the bed, was Moxy. Moxy froze, knowing she was supposed to be a toy now – silent, still and steady.

The little girl picked her up and studied her. She felt the nubby thing on the top of Moxy's head, and she peered into Moxy's buggy eyes. She seemed to be most concerned about Moxy's three big teeth. Moxy tried to stay still, but she'd never been so nervous. She wanted the girl to love her. She wanted her to think she was special and unique, even though she knew....

The girl smiled a goofy three-tooth smile. She must've just lost some baby teeth, and her big teeth were growing in now, and everything looked a bit different than Moxy expected. She hugged Moxy close to her chest, and Moxy tried hard not to cry. Her child loved her – truly loved her. She could feel it in every inch of her plush body.

Yes, Moxy thought. *It doesn't get better than this.*